W9-AOC-547

First published in Switzerland under the title *Der Stern*.


First published in the United States, Great Britain, Canada,
Australia, and New Zealand in 2001 by North-South Books,
an imprint of Nord-Süd Verlag AG, Gossau Zürich, Switzerland.

Distributed in the United States by North-South Books Inc., New York.

Library of Congress Cataloging-in-Publication Data is available.
A CIP catalogue record for this book is available from The British Library.
ISBN 0-7358-1509-7 (trade binding) 10 9 8 7 6 5 4 3 2 1
ISBN 0-7358-1510-0 (library binding) 10 9 8 7 6 5 4 3 2 1
Printed in Germany

For more information about our books, and the authors and artists
who create them, visit our web site: www.northsouth.com

*Ute Blaich* **The Star**

*Illustrated by Julie Litty*

*Translated by Sibylle Kazeroid*

A Michael Neugebauer Book
North-South Books / New York / London



INNISFIL PUBLIC LIBRARY
P.O. BOX 7049
INNISFIL, ON L9S 1A8

The night was bitterly cold.
Owl and Raven sat in a plum bush.
“It's beastly cold,” cawed Raven.
“Terribly cold,” agreed Owl, ruffling his feathers. He looked sadly at the snowy landscape. Was anything out there?

“Horribly cold,” came a whisper. “Not a single cranberry. Nothing . . .” It was White Grouse.

“Don’t complain, little White Grouse,” said Owl. “You should be used to such cold weather.”

“Not at all,” said White Grouse. “You’re thinking about my relatives in Greenland. I’m from here. It’s so icy that my beak is freezing.”

A cracking sound in the bush made all three stand still. Suddenly, Sheep stood before them in the moonlight.

"Well, Sheep?"

Sheep shook the snowflakes from his thick fur and looked curiously at the plum bush branches.

"Is there anything to eat here?"

"Nothing, not even a mouse," answered Owl, annoyed.

Sheep looked around, astonished. "Owl, you're joking," he said. "I see Mouse right there in front of you."

It was true. Mouse had practically sunk into the snow, and behind her lay a trail of tiny, dainty footprints. Mouse kept her distance from Owl and anxiously looked around for an escape route. But Owl made no move to grab her.

"What is wrong, Owl, my friend?" asked Raven. "An excellent little meal is waiting . . ."

Owl slowly turned his wise head and said sharply, "You should know, Raven. Today is the 24th of December."

"Yes, and?" Raven looked at Owl blankly.

Now White Grouse was curious, too. He came closer to Owl and asked, "Yes, and what?"

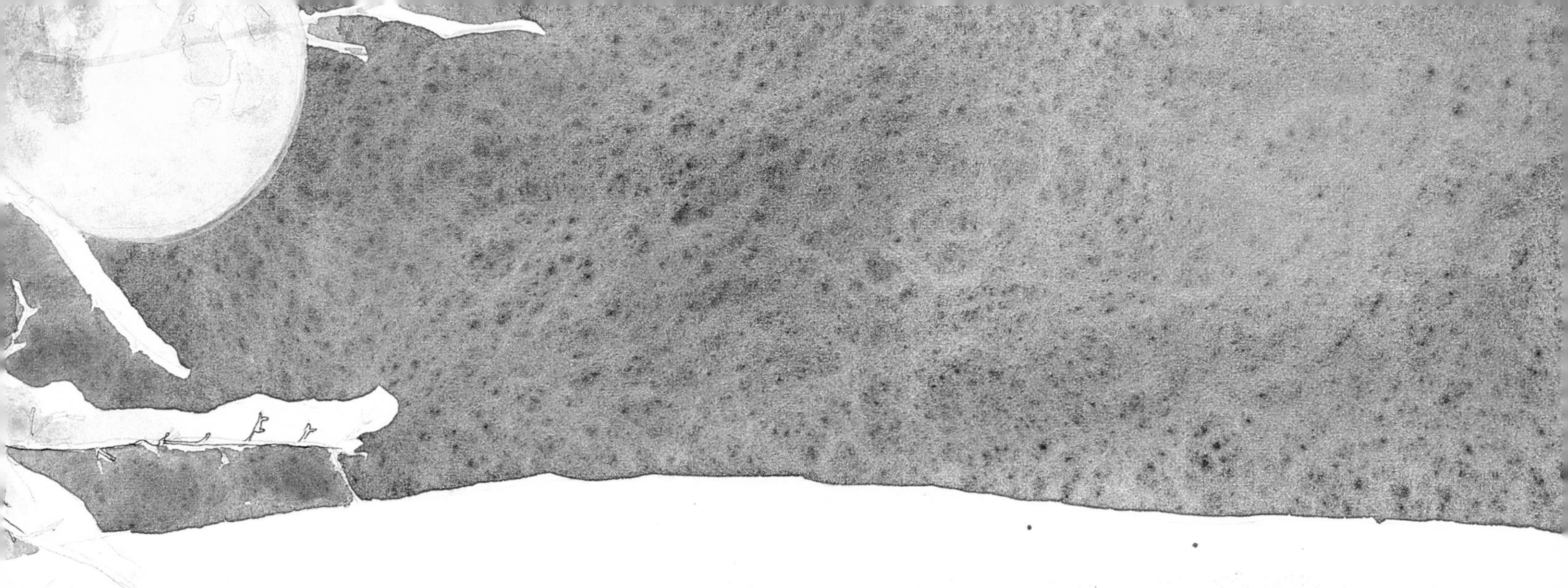

Sheep stayed where he was and pricked up his ears.
Owl asked impatiently, "Don't any of you know what this day means?"
The animals just shook their heads.
"Then look up!" said Owl.

White Grouse, Raven, Sheep, and Mouse stared intently at the sky. On that cold winter's night, the sky was clear and brilliant. Next to the moon they could see a shining, twinkling star.
"The star of Bethlehem," Owl declared.
The others just stood there, confused.
Owl smoothed his feathers and after a long pause, said,

"Bethlehem is a very special place."
"Why?" asked White Grouse.
"An important person was born there."
"What is his name?"
"Son of man."
"That's ridiculous," said Raven scornfully.
"What is a person other than a son of man? 'Son of Wolf?' 'Son of Elephant?'"

Owl shot Raven a look and said, "Well, they claim that he was not only a son of man, but also the son of God. And what made him remarkable was that he was not malicious, or vengeful, or violent, or murderous. He was a good person."

"But there are no good people," objected White Grouse. "People lie, and steal, and hunt, and kill."

"That is true," said Owl. "And that's exactly why this gentle son of man was so miraculous. He taught his fellow people about something completely new."

"What was it?"

"Love."

"What is love?" asked Mouse.
"I will explain it to you in simple terms.
I could catch you, Mouse, and eat you.
And I confess, I'd like to. But if I don't . . ."
"That is the opposite of killing and hate,"
said White Grouse.
"And it's called love," finished Sheep.
Owl listened attentively. "Well, it's more
complicated than that, dear friends. And
among people everything is tangled and
strange. But you're on the right track,
Sheep."
"And why don't people behave in a
loving way?"
"Because they always think only of
themselves. Always," said Owl.

"But because people know that they should behave better, once a year they celebrate this good person. They call the celebration Christmas, the Feast of Peace and Love."

"And for that they eat meat," added Sheep bitterly.

"That is true." Owl turned to Sheep sympathetically. "People have their own definition of peace and love."

"And after Christmas?" asked Mouse.

"People act just like before: they are deceitful, violent, and angry," said Sheep.
"All of them?" asked White Grouse, troubled.
"There are exceptions," said Owl.
Just then, the animals heard a crunching noise in the snow.

They saw two horses pulling a sleigh and heard the voices of a man and a child.

"Here's a good spot," said the child in a bright voice.

The old man heaved two bags from the sleigh and plodded through the snow. The child led the way, pointing to a spot near the plum bush. The man began clearing away the deep snow, and the child helped. They hardly spoke while they worked, but the clouds of their breath looked like puffs of smoke from an oven.

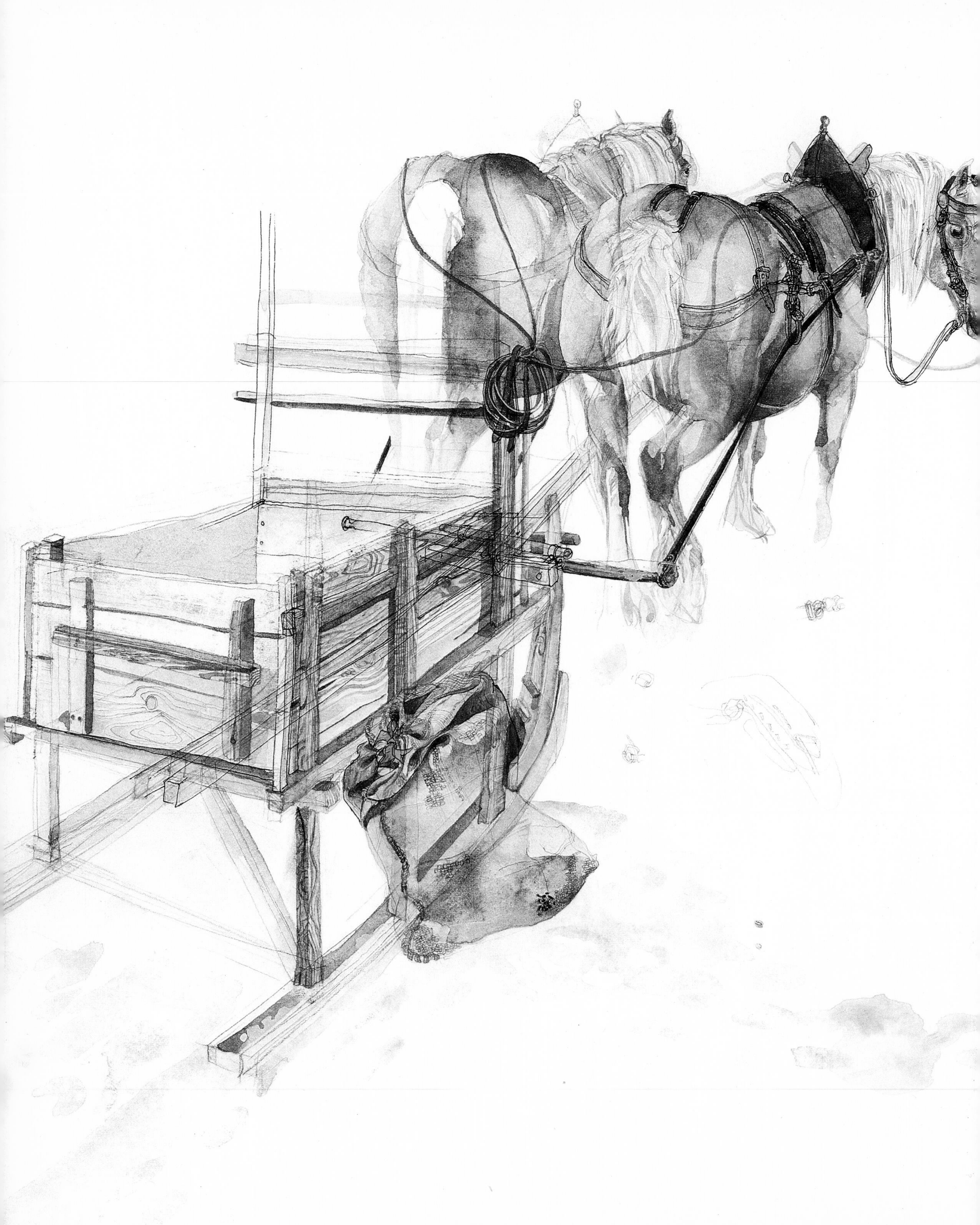

Before long, the spot was clear.
The man and the child pulled delicious treats from the two bags: corn, carrots, wheat, hay, nuts, turnips, and oats.
"Finished," said the child.
"Now the animals can celebrate Christmas, too," said the man, laughing. "Merry Christmas!"
"Merry Christmas," echoed the child.

Then the man and the child made their way back to the waiting horses. Owl, White Grouse, Raven, Sheep, and Mouse had watched this spectacle silently and intently. As soon as the sleigh was off in the distance, they came out from the plum bush.

"Well?" said Owl. "You asked me for an example of good people. They exist. You just saw for yourselves."

The moon shone more brightly than before. The animals ate in silence. Mouse walked about near Owl without fear, Sheep crunched carrots, White Grouse and Raven happily pecked at the corn and grain. Above them the star of Bethlehem shone the good news in the dark sky. As it had for two thousand years.

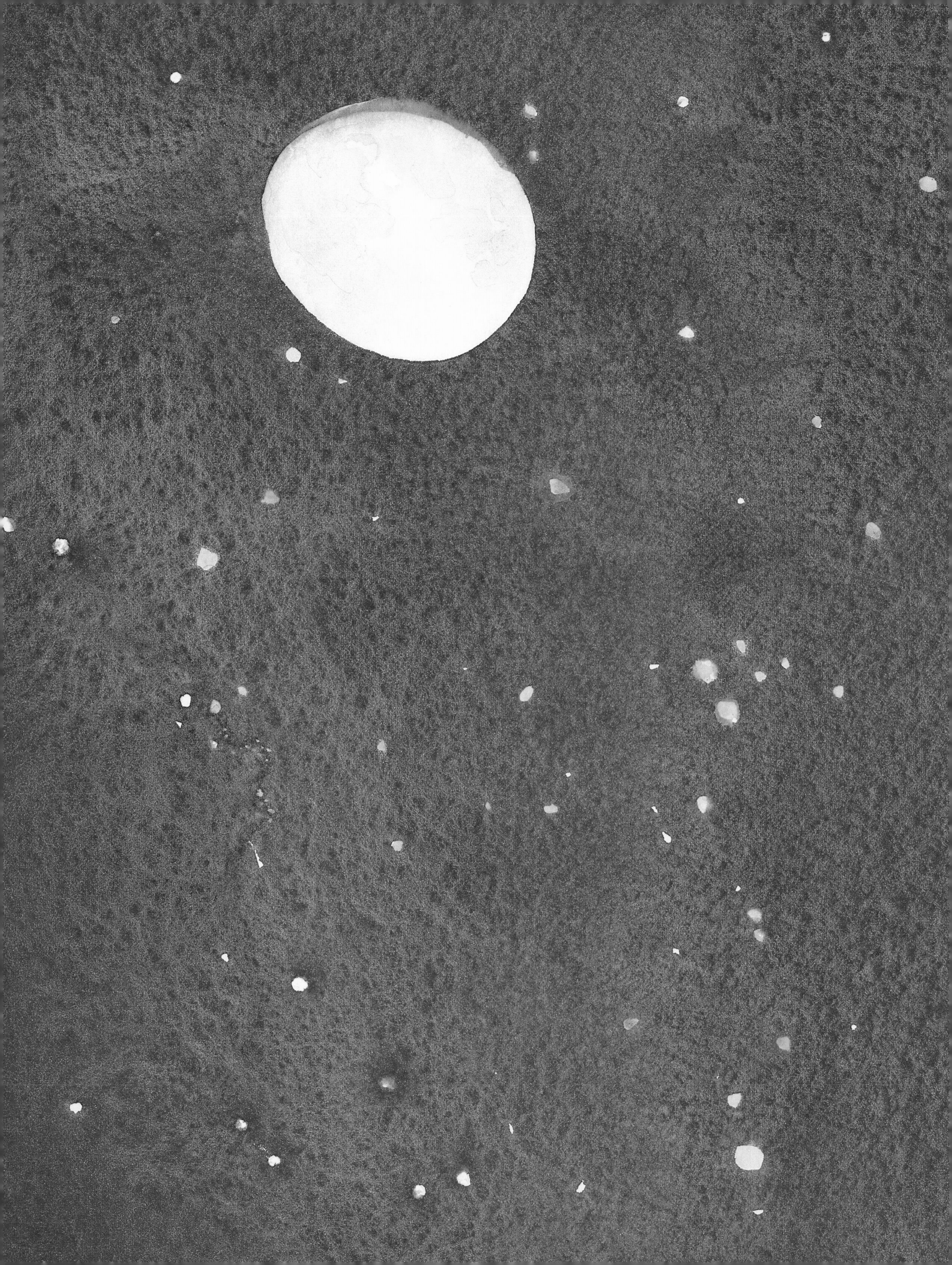